a min dition book

published by Penguin Young Readers Group

First published in German under the title SCHNEETREIBEN
Text and Illustration copyright © 2006 by Daniela Bunge
Coproduction with Michael Neugebauer Publishing Ltd., Hong Kong.
Rights arranged with "minedition" Rights and Licensing AG, Zurich, Switzerland.
Published simultaneously in Canada.
Manufactured in Hong Kong by Wide World Ltd.
Typesetting in Carmina BT by Gudrun Zapf Hesse
Color separation by Fotoriproduzione Ermanno Beverari, Verona
Library of Congress Cataloging-in-Publication Data available upon request.

ISBN 0-698-40045-3
10 9 8 7 6 5 4 3 2 1
First Impression

For more information please visit our website: www.minedition.com

THE SCARVES

Daniela Bunge

Translated by Kathryn Bishop

Every weekend I visit my grandparents.
One day when I got there, my grandfather was
standing outside by the front door with lots of
suitcases and things.
"Grandpa, are you going on a trip?" I asked.
"Well, something like that," said Grandpa.

Grandpa loaded everything into the car,
and then we took a little walk through the park.
"I'm not going to be living with Grandma for a while,"
he said. "Instead I'll have my own apartment.
Would you like to come and have a look at it?"

The new apartment was at the other end of the park, though you could almost see Grandma's apartment through the trees.

"Don't you like Grandma anymore?" I asked.

"It's not that simple," said Grandpa. "We're just so different. Your grandmother likes cats, and her favorite color is blue. She wakes me up too early in the morning. I always have to clean up after her, and she eats MY chocolate pudding. She always gets to decide what we watch on television. And she never wants to have a vacation in the mountains, like I do."

When I went to Grandma's, she had changed the whole
apartment. There didn't seem to be a sign of Grandpa left,
but there was a little cat.
"Don't you like Grandpa any more?" I asked.
"It's not that simple," said Grandma. "We're just so different.
Grandpa loves houseplants, and his favorite color is red.
He makes me crazy with his loud music. He never leaves me
any chocolate pudding, he always chooses our television
shows, and he never wants to go with me to the beach."

On Saturday I visited Grandpa, and he had bought gallons of paint —
red paint. There was cherry red, raspberry red and even tomato red.
The new apartment was going to look just like he had always wanted.
It was funny, Grandpa didn't seem sad at all. He whistled along with
songs on the radio.

On Sunday I visited Grandma, and her
apartment was now all in blue. But the
kitchen seemed kind of big without Grandpa.
Grandma had made chocolate pudding.
She could eat all she wanted now, but she
didn't seem to have any appetite.
"Are you crying?" I asked.
"No," said Grandma.
The pudding tasted kind of salty.
Grandma didn't eat one bite.

The following week Grandpa didn't get up until almost
noon. Without Grandma it was boring. He looked lonesome
and lost sitting there among his houseplants.
"Are you crying?" I asked.
"Oh, don't be silly," said Grandpa. "I'm just watching the snowflakes."
I didn't believe him.

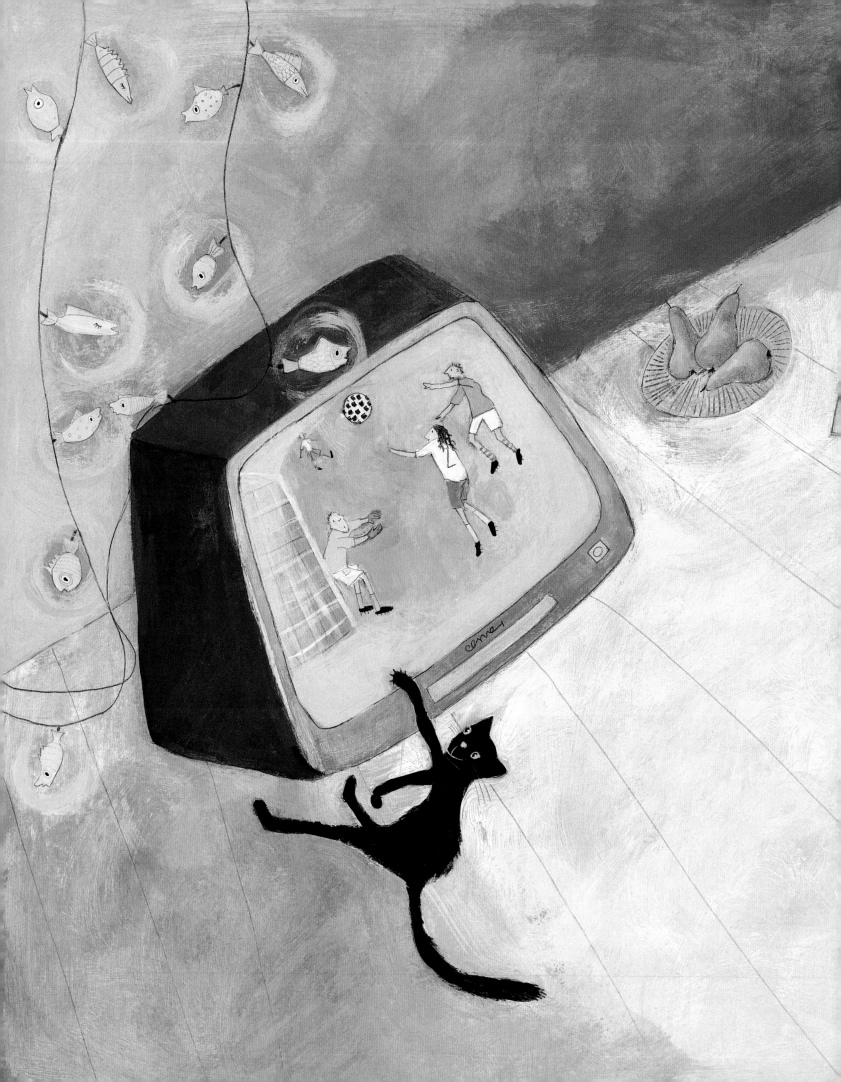

Grandma was very excited when she opened the door to let me in, but then quickly turned around and went right back to the television show she was watching. Now she could watch whatever she wanted. But she was watching Grandpa's favorite show. Since when did Grandma like soccer?

I began to wonder about Grandpa too.
At his apartment he proudly showed me his new bathing suit.
I just stared because Grandpa doesn't even know how to swim.
"You know I was thinking, I might go to the beach for a vacation,"
said Grandpa as he made swimming motions with his arms.

One day Grandma said, "I want to show you something."
Under the bed she had hidden a big box.
"I met your grandfather ice skating over 30 years ago," said Grandma
as she pulled out an old photo.
"Your grandfather was the best ice skater, and he had such rosy cheeks."
Suddenly, Grandma had red cheeks too.

When I went to Grandpa's, I asked
him, "How did you meet Grandma?"
Grandpa took down a box of pictures from
the closet.
"It was a winter's day on Little Lake. Grandma was
dancing over the ice with snowflakes in her hair.
She looked like a princess," said Grandpa, his eyes twinkling
as he stared at one of the pictures.

Grandma and Grandpa still loved each other, that was clear. Something
    had to be done! Outside it was snowing and snowing, and the lake was
        freezing over.
        Then I had an idea. I went to the big cupboard and found yarn in
            Grandma and Grandpa's favorite colors.
            Every evening I worked, and all you could hear was the clickity-
                clack of my knitting needles. Finally, when I was finished
                    I wrapped two packages— one for Grandma, and one for
                        Grandpa. Then I wrote two letters.

"Sunday afternoon, 2:30 at Little Lake. Bring your ice skates."

I secretly delivered them to the front door of each apartment.
"Oh, I hope my plan works!" I thought.

The next day I went to the park. Little Lake was in the middle of the park, but I couldn't see either of my grandparents. Then in the distance, between the snowflakes I could see a couple dancing on the ice.
It was Grandma and Grandpa with their scarves flapping in the wind.

The next weekend I rang the bell at Grandpa's apartment.
Grandma was sitting at the table, laughing. Grandpa had made chocolate
pudding for her. Her cat was there too.
"You're going to have to look after the cat," said Grandma.
"We'll be going on a trip soon, a trip to the mountains and to the beach!"
I just smiled.